Dunc Breaks the Record

OTHER YEARLING BOOKS YOU WILL ENJOY:

DUNC'S HALLOWEEN, *Gary Paulsen*
THE VOYAGE OF THE *FROG*, *Gary Paulsen*
CHOCOLATE FEVER, *Robert Kimmel Smith*
JELLY BELLY, *Robert Kimmel Smith*
MOSTLY MICHAEL, *Robert Kimmel Smith*
THE WAR WITH GRANDPA, *Robert Kimmel Smith*
HOW TO EAT FRIED WORMS, *Thomas Rockwell*
HOW TO FIGHT A GIRL, *Thomas Rockwell*
HOW TO GET FABULOUSLY RICH, *Thomas Rockwell*
UPCHUCK SUMMER, *Joel L. Schwartz*

Gary Paulsen

Dunc Breaks the Record

A YEARLING BOOK

Published by
Dell Publishing
a division of
Bantam Doubleday Dell Publishing Group, Inc.
666 Fifth Avenue
New York, New York 10103

ISBN: 0-440-40678-1

Printed in the United States of America

November 1992

10 9 8 7 6 5 4 3 2 1

OPM

Dunc Breaks the Record

Chapter · 1

"It's like this—I'll put it the same way my uncle Alfred says it—if I'd been meant to fly, I'd have feathers on my butt and my feet would fit a limb."

Amos was standing on a hillside north of town. Actually, not standing so much as digging his heels in. He was wearing a helmet and orange sunglasses with pastel frames. The helmet strap was so tight, he had to talk through clenched teeth. "I won't do it."

He was not standing alone. Dunc—Duncan—Culpepper, his best friend for life, was there with him. Well down the hill, a mile away and seemingly almost vertically below them, stood their helper and instructor, Tod Meserman.

Dunc was standing beneath a hang glider and holding its pipe frames. It was early morning—just past dawn—and though the air was fairly calm, soft breezes wafted up the hill and fluttered the cloth on the glider now and then.

"Come on, Amos. You did it at least ten times when you were taking the lessons." Dunc wiggled the glider to emphasize. "It's perfectly safe."

"I crashed."

"You didn't crash. You made a slightly early landing."

"I crashed. I went down like an anvil out of a four-story window. I hit so hard, I saw colors and drove my knees up around my ears."

Dunc sighed. "It was your second flight, and if you hadn't let go of the control bar to swat that fly, you wouldn't have cra—come down quite so fast."

"Bee. It was a bee. Not a fly. Probably a killer bee. And I crashed."

Dunc shook his head and turned to face down the hill, wiggling the glider around. "Call it what you like—it doesn't matter. This time there'll be two of us. I'll be there with you. All we have to do is launch, let the glider float down the hill to Mr. Meserman, and we'll have the record."

"The record—that's another thing. You're being a little pushy about this record business. It's not all that important."

"Not important? It's the *world* record, Amos! The longest flight ever for two boys our age on a hang glider! We'll be in all the record books."

"Big deal."

"We'll be famous."

"Right—as the first two boys our age to drop like anvils from a four-story building."

"And everybody—even Melissa—will read about us. Think of it. Melissa Hansen reading about you being a hero."

Doubt mixed with interest on Amos's face, starting a small battle with a frown between his eyes, and in a moment interest won. "Melissa . . ." Melissa Hansen had been the object of Amos's dreams, it seemed, since before he was born, before he could think. She didn't know he walked the planet, and she had never spoken to him or touched him except once when she thought he was his cousin, the skateboarder Lash Malesky, and again when she thought he was a dog because Amos was a dog.

"Sure"—Dunc nodded—"I can see it now. She's in the library, the record book is open on a table. She looks at it. Hmmm, she thinks. Hang gliders. And look, here's Amos Binder. Cool, she thinks—he's got the record. I should meet this guy."

And it worked. Amos nodded, smiled, and moved to stand with Dunc inside the framework of the glider. He slipped into the harness that would hold him while they flew. "Melissa . . ."

"All right," Dunc said, "hold the bar and run with me, and when I give the word, kick off. Just like Mr. Meserman showed us. All we have to do is glide down the hill to where he's standing, and we'll be in the record books."

"Melissa . . ."

Dunc started his run, and Amos trotted beside him.

Dunc started to run faster, and Amos picked up speed.

The glider started to lift. Just a bit at first, and then the morning breeze, which was gaining speed coming up the hill even as they ran, caught under the front of the glider.

"Now!" Dunc pushed forward on the control bar. The nose of the glider went up, and with a surge they were off the ground, flying.

"Lie out flat." Dunc kicked his legs back, and Amos copied him.

The glider wobbled a bit, but Dunc corrected with the bar, and it settled into a proper attitude and began to slide down the hill, about thirty feet off the ground.

"See?" Dunc said. He was smiling. "Isn't this great? We're just greasing on down, and then—"

They would argue later over what he had been about to say next. Dunc said he was going talk about being in the record books. Amos swore he was going to say: "—just greasing on down, and then we'll fly away and ruin our lives and everything, and die."

At first there was a natural flow to what happened.

The morning breeze coming up the hill freshened still more, and a sudden gust caught the glider. It shot up two hundred feet.

"Yalp!" Amos shouted, or something very like

a gulp that turned into a yell. "What happened?"

"No problem," Dunc said. He pulled the bar back, and the nose of the glider dropped. "It was just a little updraft."

"Mr. Meserman looks awful small down there." Amos took his hand off the bar to point. The glider wiggled. He put his hand back on the bar. "I mean *really* small."

"I just have to compensate a bit more."

"So do it. Compensate."

Dunc pulled further back on the bar. The nose dropped still more, but it didn't help.

The glider continued to climb.

"Compensate," Amos said, his voice becoming shrill. *"Compensate!"*

"I am." It was a cool morning, but Dunc was starting to sweat. Damp spots showed through his jacket. His forehead under the helmet was damp. "I'm pulling back all I dare."

"Why aren't we going down?"

"I don't know—we should be dropping fast."

"We're still climbing!"

"I know, Amos. I'm here with you, remember?"

"I can't see Mr. Meserman."

"Sure you can—there he is, by his car. See?"

"He's just a dot. A tiny dot!"

Dunc pushed sideways on the bar. The glider swooped off to the left.

"What are you doing?" Amos fought him on the bar, and the glider wobbled like a sick bat.

"I think we're caught in some kind of updraft or thermal. I thought maybe if we slid off sideways we would start down."

"We didn't." Amos's knuckles were white on the bar.

"I know."

"We're still climbing."

"I know."

"We're going to die."

"No, we're not."

"We're going to fall and fall and crash and drop and plummet and die."

"No, we're not."

"I have to go to the bathroom."

"Be quiet now."

"Bad."

"Amos—"

Even though the nose stayed down, the glider continued to climb, until even Mr.

Meserman's car—a large station wagon with a rack on top to haul the glider—couldn't be seen.

Until town, eight miles away, was lost in the blurry haze of altitude.

Up and up and up . . .

Chapter · 2

"Yes," Dunc said, nodding. "It's a thermal. That's what it is."

Amos had his eyes closed tightly, the lids jammed down. "I don't care. I'm not looking."

"Oh, heck, Amos, it's not so bad. We just got carried up a ways. As soon as we get off this thermal, we can get back down."

"That's what bothers me—the down part."

"It's all very simple." Dunc pulled himself slightly around so he could see to the rear. "The air moves up that hill, just like Mr. Meserman told us. I guess it just moves more than he thought it would, or faster. See out there off to the right—those clouds? That's what caused the wind and the thermal to come up."

"I don't see anything."

"You will if you open your eyes."

Amos opened his eyes. Then wider—so wide, they seemed to pop out of his head. "Dunc, I can't see anything! I'm blind! The altitude is making me blind!"

Dunc reached across and jerked on Amos's helmet strap. "Your helmet is in front of your eyes. Look—it's beautiful."

"It's down—everything is down from here." Amos blinked. "There is no up."

Dunc pulled the bar sideways, and the glider moved off to the right.

"What are you doing?" Amos clutched at the bar. "Don't move that way."

"It's so strange. I can turn left or right, but it won't go down. In fact, we're still climbing. I'll bet we're ten, twelve thousand feet up now. I wish I had an altimeter—I *know* we've got the record now."

All the time he talked, Amos had been strangely silent. He craned his neck around to look back, then forward. "Dunc . . ."

"Not just the distance record for two boys our age, but probably the altitude record as well."

"Dunc . . ."

"Maybe if I held the nose up a little, we'd climb still more—just to clinch it."

"Dunc!"

"You don't have to scream—I'm right next to you."

"I've been looking down."

"I know. And I'm very proud of you, conquering your fears that way."

"That's not it. I've been looking down, and I don't recognize anything."

"It all looks different from up here."

"No." Amos shook his head, his helmet wobbling in the sunlight. "I mean, we're moving. It's hard to tell from up here, but I think we're sliding sideways all the time."

Dunc studied the ground, then nodded slowly. "I think you might be right—there must be a sidewind, and we're blowing with it. I think we're moving southwest."

"Southwest," Amos said, "southwest. How fast are we going?"

Dunc shook his head. "I can't be sure. I think I read an article in the library once that said the fronts go through here at about thirty-five miles an hour."

"And we've been up here how long?"

Dunc looked at his watch. "Almost an hour—man, that's *got* to be the record! Not only distance but altitude and time—we've got them all!"

But Amos was figuring. "So we've come close to thirty-five miles, heading southwest."

Dunc nodded. "I think so—maybe. About."

"And we haven't started down yet."

"Not yet."

"This isn't good," Amos said. "Not good at all."

"What's the matter? We'll come down sooner or later."

"Think," Amos said. "You've been so caught up in this record business, you're forgetting something. We're heading southwest. We've come thirty or so miles, and we're still heading that way."

"Right—when we come down, we'll get to a phone and call home. It'll all work out."

"Except for one point—the Davis Wilderness Area starts twenty-five miles southwest of town."

"Oh." Dunc nodded. "I didn't think of that."

"And it stretches for close to eighty miles in a southwest direction."

"Almost ninety, actually," Dunc said. "I read that it was named after a guy named Milton Davis who worked hard to save some small trees or fish or something. He disappeared back in the seventies."

"You're not following me, Dunc." Amos took his hand off the bar long enough to wave a finger, then slammed it back down when the glider wiggled. "Stay with me now—we're flying in a hang glider out over a wilderness area where there isn't a phone or a road. We don't have any way to get out. We don't have any food or clothing with us. We don't even have a compass."

Dunc studied Amos for a moment, then nodded slowly. "I see your point, but I think you're worrying needlessly. We haven't started down yet. Heck, we might go all the way across the wilderness area before we come down."

But they didn't.

Chapter · 3

"Dunc, why is everything getting bigger?" Amos was looking down. "See the trees, and that river —aren't they getting bigger?"

Dunc nodded but said nothing. He was also watching the ground intently, frowning. Below them stretched miles and miles of raw wilderness—thickly wooded small mountains and rolling hills. Here and there lay a lake, cut back between hills, and across the whole of it stretched a river.

"Are we going down?" Amos looked at Dunc.

Dunc nodded. "We must have lost the thermal."

Amos looked down at the forest. He looked

forward, then back, then left and right. "I don't want to seem like a party pooper, but has it occurred to you that there is nowhere to land? I can't even see a clearing."

Dunc nodded again. "I know. I've been looking for some time now."

"Well, we'll just have to not land, that's all."

"Amos . . ."

"Keep the nose up, and we'll just keep flying."

Dunc sighed. He held the glider almost on the edge of stalling, felt it shudder, dropped the nose, and turned to the right a bit. "It doesn't work that way. When it's time to come down, it's time to come down. There's nothing I can do. Now, help me find a place to land—quick. We only have a few minutes."

He angled back to the right, then to the left.

"I don't see anything," Amos said. "Do you?"

"No."

By now, the glider had dropped low enough that they could make out individual trees and brush.

"There's nothing," Amos said. "We're going to crash in the trees."

"No." Dunc canted the bar. "We can't land in

the trees. If we lose flying speed at the tops of the trees, we still have to fall to the ground."

"There's nowhere else." Amos's voice rose to the edge of shrill.

"Only one place," Dunc said, lining the glider out. "The river."

"In the *water*?"

"We don't have any choice." Dunc moved the bar again and slowed the descent as much as he dared. Still the glider dropped, and now he could see limbs on trees, even large leaves.

The river below them was not a peaceful winding stream. It shot through cuts between hills, and here and there it had whitewater rapids. It was also not straight. Because the hills kinked it back and forth, most of the river below the glider—where Dunc would have to bring it down—was in narrow twisting cuts.

"There," Dunc said, pointing with his chin. "Right there—see where the water cuts across the face of that hill, that straight part? That's where we'll bring it in."

"Those are rapids, Dunc."

"Just out in the middle. I'm going to come in on the side. I'll just skin her in, and . . ."

He trailed off as he concentrated on flying.

He turned away from the landing spot, let the glider sink a bit, then brought it back around, lined the nose up heading back up the river and into the wind, and aimed directly at the site he'd picked for landing.

It almost went perfectly. Even Amos was impressed.

Dunc brought the glider in just as he'd said, lined the nose up on the side of the river, wobbled it down into the wind, and flared just above the water. The two boys lowered their feet until it seemed they were just about to walk on the water.

"Beautiful," Amos said. "I couldn't have done it better—"

He had been about to add the word *myself.* But he didn't get it out. He very nearly never said another word again of any kind.

Their feet hit the water almost at the same time. Amos was introduced violently to some basic laws of physics concerning fluids and gases. He found that his upper half, attached to the glider, kept moving through the air much better than his bottom half, which was in the water.

In fact the bottom half stopped dead.

"Pluummphh!"

As their bodies entered the water, the glider tried to keep flying. It couldn't, and in half a second it slammed forward and down into the water in an impact that shot water thirty feet into the air.

They were on the edge of the rapids—Dunc had brought the glider down as he said he would—but the sudden jerk forward pushed the nose of the glider out into the current.

The glider material acted in the water like a parachute, caught the full force of the river, and took off at a speed matching the current.

The boys were still attached in their harnesses. Upside down, tumbling, the hang glider thundered down the river, cartwheeling in the current, breaking spars and snapping cables, dragging Amos and Dunc end over end behind it.

Dunc grabbed at the harness and fought to get free. He clawed, missed the release, and found it again when he was upside down. Air bubbles streamed up from his nostrils. He pulled, tore free, then reached back for Amos.

And missed.

He had one glimpse of Amos, head down, eyes squinched shut, stiff as a poker under water. Then the current ripped the glider away from Dunc, and Amos disappeared downstream.

Chapter • 4

Amos was dreaming.

In the dream he was standing in the center of his living room, turned toward the door, ready to go outside, when the phone rang.

Even in the dream he had good form. He wheeled in one smooth motion and felt his legs power him, driving him off sideways at a perfect angle to grab the phone on the wall just inside the kitchen door, to get it by that all-important second ring. There was another phone on the end table in the living room, but his mind, quick as a computer, reckoned it to be nearly eight centimeters farther than the one in the kitchen.

Both legs driving, arms pumping, a little spit out the side of his mouth—classic form.

Then the cat.

"Amos!"

They didn't even have a cat. His sister Amy, whom Amos called the Dragon, was allergic to cats. But in the dream there was a cat. A big old tom, scarred and mangy, and just as Amos made the pivot it moved from beneath the dining-room table and stepped perfectly between his ankles. As the phone began the second ring, he started down. With one clawing hand he caught the phone—just as his face slammed into the carpet so hard, he felt the fabric drive through his skin. . . .

"Amos—wake up. . . ."

Amos opened his eyes.

For a moment he couldn't remember anything, and he was startled to see Dunc leaning over him wearing a helmet and apparently wrapped in some kind of red cloth.

"Dunc?"

"Oh, man, I thought you were gone this time." Dunc rolled Amos on his side. "You must have puked five gallons of water."

"What are you doing here?" Amos stared at

Dunc. "I was just going to answer the phone. . . . Oh. Oh. Now I remember. It was a dream. Man, even in my dreams I can't get to the phone."

Dunc stood. He had grabbed some of the material from the glider and pulled the glider off Amos so he could pump his chest, and he was now tangled in the cloth. He pulled it away and dropped it onto the ground. "I can't believe I found you."

"What happened?"

"You want the whole story?" Dunc asked.

"Yes."

"Well, we decided to break the record for two boys our age on a hang glider—"

"No, I remember all that. I mean in the river, with the glider. What happened?"

"We got separated. I broke loose, and the current took you on down. It was just a fluke—you got caught up on a snag that jutted out from the bank, and I saw the red of the glider cloth. Otherwise you would have been in trouble."

Amos stared at him. "This isn't trouble?"

"Well—not as much as it could have been."

"Dunc, *we* didn't decide to break the record. *You* decided to break the record, and if *you* hadn't decided to break the record, *we* wouldn't be in this fix."

"Amos—"

"Admit it."

"Amos—"

"Admit it now. It's all your fault."

"All of it?"

"Yes."

"Even the thermal?"

"Everything. Everything in the whole world that has ever gone wrong is completely and totally your fault, starting with maybe the Second World War and going right up the present time and maybe even in the future."

"All right. It's all my fault."

"Thank you—I feel much better now." Amos took his helmet off and leaned over. He wiggled his head to clear the water out of his ears, then stopped and looked up at Dunc with his head cocked. "So what do we do now?"

Dunc didn't answer right away. He took his own helmet off, pulled his jacket and T-shirt off, and wrung them out. Then he sat on a rock, pulled his shoes and pants off, and hung all his clothing on a branch to dry.

Taking it all as a suggestion, Amos did the

same. The two boys sat in their underwear on a large, flat rock overlooking the river and let the sun bake them. The glider, or what was left of it, lay in a crumpled mass to their rear.

"Well?" Amos said.

"Well what?" The sun was warm, and Dunc felt a strange urge to just close his eyes and sleep. *Maybe,* he thought, *it will all go away if I sleep—maybe it's all a dream.*

"Well, what are we going to do?"

"I haven't the faintest idea."

"Stop it, Dunc—you always have ideas. That's how it works. Your beady little brain is always cooking. That's why we get into all the trouble we get into—because you're all the time having ideas."

"Not this time. It's like my brain stopped when we hit the water. I remember seeing you head off downstream, and I was scared you would drown, and somehow I got to shore and ran after you—but there wasn't any thinking going on."

"Dunc . . ."

"Honest. And it doesn't seem to be happening now, either. It's just a blank in there." He scratched his stomach where a tree limb had bruised him while he was swimming to shore. "Isn't it nice, just sprawling out in the sun? Kind of like being a lizard or something."

"Are you out of your mind?" Amos sat up and looked down at Dunc. "We have crashed in the middle of a wilderness with no kind of survival gear or food. Nobody knows where we are. We could die. In fact, we probably *will* die. So think of something!"

Dunc opened one eye and studied Amos. "You make it sound worse than it is."

"The heck I do!" Amos looked at his digital watch, which amazingly was still working. "We've got two, maybe three hours until dark. Dark is when things happen out here in the wilderness. Bad things. Big things move around and eat little things when it gets dark. I saw that on the Discovery Channel. And we definitely classify as little things."

Dunc sighed. "Really, Amos—it'll all work out. Mr. Meserman saw us go and probably went for help. They'll start searching for us pretty soon. I'll bet there are planes and helicopters starting up right now—we'll probably be home in half an hour. So just lay back and enjoy the sun."

"You really think so?"

"No problem—you'll be home watching television and eating chips and dip in a couple of hours."

It was the second-wrongest thing Dunc had ever said.

Chapter • 5

Dark didn't come gradually, the way it does in movies and on television.

One moment it was light and sunny, and the boys were relaxing on the rock drying their clothes. Then it seemed the next minute it was stone dark, so dark they couldn't see their hands in front of their faces.

Amos had been wrong about big things coming to eat them. No big things bothered them at all. What came to eat them were small things. Millions of them.

Mosquitoes.

And they didn't come slowly.

All in one motion, it seemed, it became dark.

Amos turned to Dunc and said, "Didn't it get dark fas—"

That was as far as he got before the air was filled with the shrill whine of clouds of mosquitoes. And each and every little one of them was hungry.

Dunc tried slapping them. He killed ten or twenty, but then another eight or nine thousand took their places. He put his jacket on and pulled it up over his ears.

Amos went completely crazy. "They're after me, they're after me—little vampires!" he screamed, and ran into the river.

Dunc heard the splash and pulled his jacket down, but it was so dark, he couldn't see anything. "Amos?"

He heard a bubbling sound, then a *whoosh.* "I'm here—in the shallow part next to the bank. They can't get you under water."

"You can't stay in the river all night."

"Watch me! If I stay up there, I wouldn't have enough blood for a blood test by morning."

Dunc pulled his jacket back up, zipped it over his head, and talked through the cloth. "I can't understand it—they should have come for us by now."

There was another *whoosh*—something like a whale blowing—as Amos held his breath and went under water to get rid of the mosquitoes around his head. He came up in fifteen seconds. "It's like the book."

"What book?"

"I read this book—*Hatchet.* About a kid who crashes in the wilderness. He had trouble with mosquitoes too."

"What did he do?"

"He made a fire. The smoke scared them away or something."

"How can we make a fire? We don't have any matches. And if we had them, they'd be wet."

"He had this hatchet, see, and this porcupine attacked him and he threw the hatchet, and it hit some rocks and made sparks. . . ." Amos trailed off and went under, then came up again. "So he beat on a rock with the hatchet until he got a fire. Then he ate raw turtle eggs and berries and puked a lot."

"And this is supposed to help us?"

"Well. It worked for him—Brian, his name was—and he made it all right. He went fifty-four days."

"Amos, we don't have a hatchet. We don't

have anything except our clothes and a busted-up hang glider and just about every mosquito in the world."

Amos sighed, went under, came up. "I'm just trying to help."

There was a soft rustling sound in the brush, a scuffle, then quiet.

"Dunc?"

Dunc didn't answer.

"Come on, Dunc, this is no time to fool around."

Silence, except for the whine of mosquitoes.

Amos crawled out of the river and felt around in the darkness. "Dunc?"

He swung his hands, then moved across and back across the clearing along the river where Dunc had been sitting.

"Dunc?"

There was no answer. It took him a full five minutes of searching, running back and forth in his underwear, to realize that not only was Dunc gone, but so was everything else—the hang glider and his clothes.

Everything.

"Dunc?"

Chapter · 6

It was the second-longest night in Amos's entire life. (The longest was the night he turned into a werepuppy and had to fight two pit bulls, a werewolf, and a volleyball net and nearly ate his own foot.)

The mosquitoes did not let up. In fact, they seemed to be mad that Dunc was gone, and twice as many homed in on Amos's bare skin.

Amos moved back into the river and crouched under water. He rolled on his back and put everything under except his nose and mouth—which the mosquitoes quickly found and tore into. Periodically he ducked under water or sloshed water in his face. He spent the night ducking, sloshing, and spitting out dead mosquitoes, then repeating the process in the cold water for a time that seemed longer than the history of the human race. Finally, finally, the sky began to turn gray, and the sun at last crawled up.

With daylight the mosquitoes went back to wherever they hid and Amos pulled himself out of the river. He was nearly blue, so cold his teeth chattered. He found a rock above the river where the sun could get at him, and he pulled himself up to sit in the warmth.

He lay back and thought of what to do, thinking out loud. "It's all pretty simple—just like the book. First I've got to take stock. So—I've got a pair of underwear shorts, a body that looks like a prune, and—"

He looked around, down at his body. "And that's it. Underwear and prune body, and Dunc is gone."

He knew he would have to start looking for Dunc, and he fully intended to stand and do that very thing, but the sun was so warm, so comforting, that it seemed to bake the wet and cold out of his body. His eyes closed, opened once, closed again, and he was sound asleep.

Another phone dream took him.

This time he was just about to leave the front door of the house when the phone rang.

He wheeled and dropped into a leaping run in one smooth motion with absolutely flawless form—an easy ten, if anybody had been keeping form score—but Scruff, his dog, was lying there. If somebody was being kind, they would say Amos and Scruff weren't compatible—if they were being honest they'd say that Scruff had hated the ground Amos walked on ever since an accident with a hot burrito. Even in the dream Scruff didn't like him.

Amos's foot came down on Scruff's tail, Scruff rose like a wolf and sunk his teeth into Amos's leg, and pulled the leg over to the side. Amos had been going nearly at terminal velocity, and he hit the wall, skipped sideways, plowed through the stand his mother had put in the entry hall for people's hats even though people didn't wear hats, ricocheted sideways, and drove his head completely through the wall next to the kitchen door. . . .

And he woke up.

He was not alone.

Sitting at the end of the rock where he was sleeping was a Neanderthal man.

It took a full second for this to register with Amos. Part of him was still spitting drywall out of his mouth and shaking Scruff off his leg.

The Neanderthal man bared his teeth and made a growling sound.

"Yahhhh!" Amos screamed, and tried to scrabble away on his back. He forgot that he had climbed four feet to get on the rock in the first place, and he fell backward and down and drove the top of his head into another rock with the full force of his body.

I wish I'd paid more attention to that kung fu class I took, he thought when he saw the Neanderthal man coming over the top of the rock at him.

Then he thought nothing at all.

Chapter · 7

Amos opened his eyes slowly. It was dark except for an eerie blue light, and musty smelling. This time it hadn't been a dream. This time there'd been nothing but a crashing pain and then unconsciousness.

Things, he thought, *are improving.*

Then he remembered the Neanderthal man and jerked to a sitting position. Or tried to sit.

"Ohhh . . ." His head felt as if it were coming apart.

"Just take it easy—you took a bad fall."

Amos turned to see Dunc kneeling next to him. "What . . . ?"

"It's complicated," Dunc said, shaking his head. "How much do you remember?"

"Start at the beginning." Amos lay back and closed his eyes. His head was throbbing.

"Well, we decided to break the record for two boys our age on a hang glider—"

"Dunc."

"Oh—okay. You remember flying over the wilderness area—and by the way we *did* break the record, about six records."

"I remember that. And crashing. And you deserting me. And mosquitoes. And a Neanderthal man."

"Milt."

"What?"

Dunc sighed. "That was Milt."

"A Neanderthal man named Milt?"

Dunc shook his head. "He's not a Neanderthal man—at least, I don't think he is. His name is Milt, and he's a hermit or something. We're in his cave. I saw his name written on the wall."

Amos sat up again and looked around. They were in a large cave, almost a grotto. The blue light came up from water along one wall, which Amos figured must be the way in. And the way out. By squinting, he could just make out a very high ceiling and the front and side walls. Something—rain or bits of damp dirt—kept falling from the ceiling and he felt it in his hair. It was impossible to see the back wall—the cave just disappeared in the darkness.

"It goes back forever," Dunc said, watching Amos look around. "I checked."

There was junk all over the place—boards and crates and boxes and bits of rags. A complete rubber raft sat in the middle of the room on the floor, and across it lay two fishing rods. The hang glider lay by the side wall, dumped in a heap. Amos could just make out his own clothes near the wreckage, also dumped in a heap. Everything seemed to be covered in a layer of dirty gunk—even the hang glider and the clothes.

"What's all over everything?" Amos asked. "And why does it smell like that parrot has been here?"

"Everything is covered with guano," Dunc said. "That's why it smells."

"Iguana—isn't that a big lizard?"

"Not *iguana,* guano. That's the name for bat poop. The ceiling is filled with bats. Thousands and thousands of them. That's what's falling on you."

Amos looked up, then quickly brought his face down. "You mean thousands of bats are going to the bathroom on me?"

Dunc nodded. Amos moved to the side and took up the cloth from the hang glider and covered himself with it.

"Don't do that, Amos."

"Do what?"

"Don't touch the hang glider. It's his."

"What's his? Who?"

"The glider. It belongs to Milt. See, some of the things are his and some are ours—well, I guess they're all his now—and if you touch the things that are his, he gets all upset."

Amos closed his eyes, shook his head, and opened them. "Look, Dunc, is all this supposed to make sense to me? Because if it is, I'm in deep trouble or maybe I got hit harder than I thought. I mean, I don't even know how I got here. And where is the beast from the wilderness—Milt? And how do you know all this?"

Dunc held up his hand. "I don't know for sure where he is or how long he'll be gone. Sometimes he goes out for a minute or two, then he might be gone for an hour. As to how you got here, Milt brought you—the same as me. We were talking in the dark, remember? Well, the next thing I knew, I had a hand over my mouth, and he carried me off, dragged me under water and up in here."

"So why didn't you run off when he came back for me?"

"It's not that easy. I tried to get away three or four times, but he waited just outside the cave and caught me. He didn't hurt me or anything—just carried me back in here. Then when you came and were out cold, I didn't feel right about leaving without you."

"How long have we been here?" Amos looked at his wrist, but his watch was gone. "And where's my watch?"

"You were out most of the day. It's late afternoon now. Milt has your watch. It's—it's sort of his now. Except that you can get it back. Well, maybe you can get it back."

Amos nodded. "Well, good. All that makes sense to me now. We've been kidnapped by a wilderness monster named Milt who put us where bats can poop on us and owns all the things we used to own but maybe we can get them back and even though he isn't here we're not allowed to run away." He paused, took a breath. "You know what I think?"

"What?"

"I think you're just about as wacky as this Milt guy. And I'm not going to wait around to see who's worse—it's time to leave."

He stood and dusted bat guano off his shoulders and hair, moved to his clothes, and pulled them on.

Dunc joined him and started to dress but shook his head. "You'll see. We won't even get our clothes on. I mean, I've tried this before."

He was wrong.

They did get their clothes on. As a matter of fact they were totally dressed, and Amos was at the edge of the pool ready to dive in and swim out to where the light shined the brightest.

The light suddenly went out as something blocked the entrance, and in a great shower of splashing water, Milt appeared in the pool just in front of Amos.

"See?" Dunc said. "I told you."

Milt was carrying a spear, and on the end of it wiggled a fresh trout. He pushed the trout toward Amos's face two or three times.

"He's telling you to eat," Dunc said. "He wants you to eat the fish."

Amos hesitated only a second before hunger took over. He grabbed the fish and moved back by the rubber raft.

"Raw?" Dunc asked. "You're going to eat it raw?"

Amos looked up, his eyes questioning. "Unless you've got a Twinkie."

Dunc shook his head, and Amos nodded and bit into the fish.

Chapter · 8

After giving the fish to Amos, Milt shook himself dry and moved to stand near the raft. He was dressed in a ragged pair of shorts and made no effort to avoid the dropping bat guano.

Amos took the fish out of his mouth. "It doesn't taste quite as good as it looks. Is there some way we can cook it?"

Dunc shook his head. "I don't know. I haven't seen him cook anything."

"Does he talk at all or understand what we're saying?" Amos turned to Milt and spoke slowly. "Do-you-have-a-stove-and-a-frying-pan?"

Milt crouched, watching him, a quiet smile on his face.

"Do-you-know-what-I'm-saying?"

There was no indication that Milt understood, and no indication that he *didn't* understand either. Nothing.

"I haven't heard him talk," Dunc said. "But I think he knows what's going on."

"What I think is this guy is about three sandwiches short of a picnic," Amos said, shrugging, slapping the trout against his leg. "I mean, there's nobody home up there in the old bean."

"Maybe so."

"What's to keep us from just saying so long and walking out of here?"

"Him. I tried it."

"Well, I haven't. And I'm going to." He threw the fish on the ground, waved at Milt, and stepped toward the edge of the water that led out.

The effect was immediate and so fast, it was hard to see. Amos was halfway into the second step when Milt seemed to vanish from where he had been sitting and reappear in front of Amos. He did something with his hands and arms, and Amos was turned back, standing exactly as he had been standing, looking at Dunc and holding the fish.

"See?" Dunc said.

"How did he do that?"

"I don't know. It's something about how he uses his hands and arms and things. He seems to flow from one place to another, and you don't get to see it." Dunc sighed and moved to stand next to Amos. "I tried three or four times to leave, and it was always the same. I just wound up back where I started from."

"Look"—Amos pointed at Milt with the fish—"you don't understand. This is wrong. You're holding us against our will, and if you don't let us go, we'll turn you in to the proper authorities. Now we're going to go, and you're not going to do anything to stop us. Come on, Dunc."

Amos turned, took a step, and the same thing happened. He was back where he started from—unhurt, almost untouched. Just moved. And Milt crouched next to the raft, smiling quietly.

"If he does that again, I'm going to get mad," Amos said.

Milt turned suddenly, moved to the side wall of the cave where there were some boxes stacked, and rummaged for a moment. He returned with a checkerboard and a box of checkers.

"Uh-oh," Dunc said. "He wants to play checkers."

"What?" Amos turned.

"He loves checkers. But he plays for things. Maybe that's how he owns all the stuff in here. Maybe he won it."

"Dunc—are you all right?"

"I had to play him three games and he won all my clothes and the glider. He's incredible—you can't beat him. Now he wants to play you."

Milt set the board on a box in front of Amos and went to the pile of Amos's clothes. He brought them over and dumped them in a pile next to the board, then motioned Amos to sit. Then he went to a box on the other side of the raft and came back with a candle in a glass jar, which he lighted and put down next to the board.

Amos slowly knelt in front of the board, and Milt quickly put all the pieces in place. Milt hid two in his palms behind his back, then held his clenched hands out.

Amos picked the right hand.

Milt opened it to show a black checker. He turned the board so that Amos had black, and he motioned for Amos to make a move.

Amos moved a checker. He looked up at Dunc. "This is completely crazy. I mean, yesterday morning we were hang gliding, and I was waiting to go on a rafting trip with Melissa and . . ." He trailed off as Milt moved one of his men.

Amos studied the board. He moved one of his men.

Milt moved.

Amos moved.

Dunc yawned.

Milt moved.

Dunc yawned again. His eyes closed.

Amos moved.

Milt moved.

Chapter · 9

"King me, sucker!"

It was a loud yell, and it snapped Dunc out of his sleep. He had been dreaming of a hamburger. Not eating it, just watching it cook, sizzling in the pan with a piece of cheese on top of it and two pieces of bacon. For part of a second he couldn't remember where he was, and he kept smelling the hamburger cooking.

Then his eyes opened.

"You're dead now—I've got a king in back of your lines! I'll shred you! I'll tear you to pieces!"

Dunc sat up. Amos and Milt were still by the rubber boat with the checkerboard on a box, hunched over, except there were some differences. Everything in the cave—all the boxes, the rubber raft, the fishing rods, the clothing, everything—was in a huge pile behind Amos.

Milt sat in his shorts, covered with hair but nothing else.

The smell hadn't gone away—the smell of something cooking. It was so real, Dunc could even hear the sound of sizzling. He shook his head. It was still there. Then he saw it. A small fire had burned down to coals, and a pan of something was cooking on it.

"Amos?" Dunc said. "Is that something cooking?"

Amos didn't look up. He ignored Dunc and concentrated on the game.

"Amos?"

Amos looked up quickly, irritated at the interruption. "What?"

"Is that something cooking?"

"Well, of course it is. There's some trout and Spam in the pan, and some freeze-dried hash browns. I saved some for you. Milt and I already ate."

"Milt and you already ate—"

"Well, I had to let him use the stove and borrow some Spam, or he would have had to go out for another fish. But yes, we already ate. You've been asleep for hours."

Amos stopped talking as Milt jumped two pieces, grinned, and motioned for Amos to give him a king.

"See?" Amos said. "You bothered me, and he got a king. Now I'll be all day destroying him."

He turned back to the game and ignored Dunc again.

Dunc moved over to the pan that was cooking on the bed of coals. It was covered with a lid, which was just as well because the lid was covered with bat guano. *Everything* was covered with bat guano.

In the pan lay about a quarter of the trout, several pieces of Spam, and a generous plop of hash browns. There was also a large spoon—the kind the army uses in mess gear that shows up in surplus stores. For about half a second Dunc hesitated, thinking of who might have used the spoon before him. Then he shrugged and dug in. It took him three minutes flat to eat everything in the pan except the trout bones.

"Bingo!" Amos yelled from the board. "You

fell right into my trap—you're mine! I now own your shorts."

Dunc moved back to the board. Amos was leaning back on his haunches looking triumphantly at Milt, who was crouched on his feet.

"You've won his shorts?" Dunc said.

"You bet." Amos nodded. "That'll teach him to mess with the checker master."

"Checker master?"

Amos nodded. "I'm deadly. It comes from when I was small. You know my uncle Alfred, who picks at his feet all the time?"

Dunc nodded.

"Well, he used to make me play checkers with him until I beat him. And he's really good at checkers. The thing is, he'd sit there and pick between his toes while we played. Pick, pick, pick—and it smelled. It was enough to make you throw up. My only chance was to get good enough to beat him so I could get away from him."

"And now you're the checker master," Dunc said. "I didn't even know it."

Amos cocked his head. "I'm a mysterious kind of guy."

"I couldn't come close to beating him." Dunc

pointed in back of Amos. "And now you've won all this?"

Amos nodded. "Everything in the room is mine, including his shorts."

All this time Milt had been crouched, watching them in silence. Now he stood and started to take off his shorts.

"That's all right." Amos held up his hand. "You can keep them—for hygiene."

Amos put the pieces back into the small box, folded the board, and put it all on his pile.

"You won the board too?" Dunc asked.

Amos tapped his temple. "It's all up here, Dunc—checker master. It's all here." He turned to Milt. "So since the gaming is over and there doesn't seem to be any reason to be here, I guess we could take *our* stuff and put it in *our* boat and head on down the river for civilization." He turned toward the entrance.

Milt jumped to his feet, and for a moment it seemed he would make the funny moves and stop Amos.

Instead he whirled and moved to the dark at the side of the cave. He hunched over scrabbling in the dirt, then came back and held something out to Amos.

It seemed to be a metal bar, a piece of steel, until the light from the candle hit it.

It shone a deep, bright yellow.

"It's gold," Dunc said. "It looks like gold."

Chapter • 10

Amos and Dunc looked at the bar for a long time.

For a whole lifetime.

The blue light from the water in the grotto entrance mixed with flickering light from the candle in the jar and the shining yellow of the bar and seemed to make it come alive.

"It *is* gold," Amos whispered. "Real gold."

Milt nodded and held the bar out to Amos. It was heavy enough that he had to strain to hold it forward.

"I don't believe it," Dunc said. He moved forward. "It must be painted lead or something. Can I see it?" He held his hand out for the bar, and Milt handed it to him. His arm dropped like a shot when the weight hit it, and he quickly used his other hand to catch it and bring it up. He examined the bar closely, holding it to better catch the light from the candle.

"It must weigh twenty pounds. And look—there's something here, something stamped in the end." He turned the end of the bar to the light and read.

"What is it?" Amos had been leaning forward, and he was so far off balance that he nearly fell.

" 'One seven six four,' " Dunc read slowly. " 'Seventeen sixty-four.' "

"Pirate gold," Amos said. His hands came out and took the bar. He held it softly, like a mother holding a baby. "We're always looking for pirate gold, and here it is."

"In the middle of the wilderness?" Dunc shook his head. "I doubt it." He turned to Milt. "Where did you get it? Where did it come from?"

Milt looked at Dunc, at Amos, at the bar of gold, and said nothing. He waved at the pile of gear in back of Amos and the checkerboard by the candle.

"He wants," Dunc said softly, "to play you a

game of checkers for the bar against all the gear."

Milt nodded, smiling.

Amos was still staring at the gold. He spoke in a hushed, reverent voice. "How much is it worth—the gold?"

Dunc thought out loud. "It's hard to be exact without scales. Say gold is four hundred dollars an ounce, and there are sixteen ounces in a pound—that makes each pound worth sixty-four hundred dollars. If the bar weighs twenty pounds, it's worth about a hundred and twenty-eight thousand."

Amos swallowed. "Dollars?"

Dunc nodded.

"I'd have a hundred and twenty-eight thousand dollars if I played?" Amos asked.

"Well, you would if you did it—if you played him. But of course you're not going to do that."

"I'm not?" For the first time, Amos took his eyes off the gold. "I can beat him with my eyes closed. Are you out of your mind?"

"No." Dunc leaned forward and whispered into Amos's ear. "But he might be. Do you think it's fair to take advantage of him just because you can play checkers better than he can?"

"Yes." Amos's voice was firm. "Absolutely." He looked at Dunc. "He kidnapped us, remember?"

"Well—not really. I think maybe he was just lonely or something and wanted us to be company. He didn't really hurt us or anything. I'm kind of starting to like him." Dunc shook his head again. "I really don't think it would be fair for you to take all this stuff and then take his last bar of gold."

Here Milt held up his hands and shook his head violently.

"See?" Dunc said. "He doesn't want to play."

But Milt kept shaking his head and waving.

"No," Amos said, "that's not it. He's telling us it isn't his last bar of gold. There are more, aren't there?"

Milt nodded. He picked up the jar with the candle and beckoned them to follow him to a flat rock the size of a small tabletop at the side of the cave. He knelt and set the bar down and put his hands on the rock. With a sudden springing movement of his arms the rock slid sideways.

"Oh." Amos whispered. "Oh my my my my . . ."

Beneath the rock was a rectangular dug-out

storage hole. Nestled there, not wrapped or covered, was a stack of shiny bars exactly like the one the boys had seen.

"How"—Amos's voice squeaked and he coughed—"how many are there?"

Dunc pointed with his finger and counted. "Eight, nine, ten, eleven. I think. Unless there are more underneath."

Milt smiled and shook his head.

"Eleven," Dunc repeated. "Eleven bars."

"Eleven," Amos said quietly, "times one hundred and twenty-eight thousand . . ."

Dunc knew where he was going. "Just over a million, three hundred thousand dollars."

Amos smiled. "Isn't math fun—you know, when it's about something like gold bars?" He laughed. "And you were worried that he couldn't afford to play me a game of checkers for one."

Dunc sighed. "Amos, it doesn't matter if he's got a hundred bars. It's still not right to take unfair advantage of someone this way."

"Sometimes," Amos hissed, "sometimes you let your rules get in the way of what's right."

"Amos."

"You sound like my mother the time I didn't

tip over Mr. Macruthers's garbage can only he said I did only I didn't and finally I had to take the blame anyway even though I didn't tip it. At least not that time."

"Amos."

Amos's eyes brightened. "Maybe we could cut the bar in half and only be half wrong."

"Amos."

"But it's *gold,* Dunc—real *gold.*"

"Amos."

It was still not easy. Amos clutched the gold bar, his hands tight. His eyes were first on the shining yellow metal and then on Dunc, then back on the bar. At long last he leaned back and sighed. "I guess you're right. I mean, I think you're wrong, but you're right. I mean you're rightly wrong or wrongly right. Oh, heck—I don't know what I mean."

He held the bar out to Milt. "Quick. Before I change my mind."

Milt looked at the bar, at Dunc, at Amos, and then shook his head.

"Really," Amos said. "Sometimes Dunc makes me so mad, I could spit fire, but he's right. Take it. It wouldn't be fair."

Milt studied them a moment longer, then held his finger against his cheek and laughed. "Oh, man—like, this is so far-out, I can't believe it. You guys are like, honest, really honest."

Chapter • 11

"You can talk!" Amos was so surprised, he dropped the gold bar—though he caught it before it hit the ground.

Milt nodded. "Been doing it since I was like, three, four years old. It's a far-out way to communicate, although not as karma oriented as some. You know, like beams or harmonies or with music. Oh, man, I really dig music. Like, you can say so many beautiful things with music that won't come out with words. Don't you like, you know, like music?"

The boys stood speechless. Having started to talk, Milt seemed not to be able to stop.

"Like, it's so, so groovy that you didn't think it was fair to take the gold. I mean, you're probably going to have like, maybe ten or twelve good incarnations because of, you know, like, your generosity. It's so beautiful, so beautiful, man. . . ."

He paused to take a breath, and Dunc cut in. "How long have you been here?"

Milt held up his hands and counted his fingers, then went down to his toes, counted them, then started over on his fingers, and finally shrugged. "Time is like, relative—how old are the Mamas and the Papas?"

"Who?" Dunc frowned.

"Like, the rock group—you know, the Mamas and the Papas. How old are they?"

"I never heard of them."

"How about Donovan?"

"Never heard of him."

"The Monkees, the Byrds, the Groundhogs?" Milt's face looked worried.

Dunc looked at Amos. Both boys shook their heads.

"The Animals?" Milt was desperate now. "You've heard of them, right?"

"No." Dunc sighed. "All of those are from before our time."

"How about bugs," Amos offered. "You've talked about birds and animals."

"The Crickets?" Milt brightened. "They were like, solid, man!"

More head shakes.

"The Roaches?" Milt asked. "Oh, man, wait—the Beatles?"

Both boys nodded.

"Uncle Alfred told me about them. They were from England." Amos gestured with the gold bar. "Everybody said they were cool."

"Right," Milt said. "Weird hair—like bowl cuts. Far-out. So how old are the Beatles?"

Dunc sighed. "They don't exist any longer. They broke up before we were born."

Milt nodded, satisfied. "That's how long I've been here. Since back then. I took my vow of silence and headed into the wilderness then."

Dunc rubbed his head, thinking. He felt the bat guano and took his hand down. "I remember reading something about them. That was maybe 1965 or 1966. You've been here twenty-seven years?"

Milt shrugged. "Time, you know—it stretches. Seasons come and, you know—go."

"And you've been alone all that time, with no outside contact?"

Milt nodded. "Rafting trips come through and, you know, I sneak in and get food from them, but my karma is so strong, they never see me."

"That's where all this stuff comes from," Dunc said. "From rafting trips?"

Milt nodded.

"And the boat?"

Milt shook his head. "I only take food, surplus food. The boat came by on its own one day early this summer. I guess somebody lost it."

Amos shook his head. "How come if you took a vow of silence and wanted to be alone, you took us, and now you're talking to us?"

"Oh, wow, man—like, if I'd left you out there, the mosquitoes would have killed you both. I brought you in here to get you away from them. I took him first, but when I went back for you, I couldn't find you until daylight."

"I was in the water."

Dunc interrupted. "How come you talked—broke your vow of silence?"

"Like, you're honest. I swore there were no honest people left—just people who wanted to ruin, you know, like, the earth. I did some demonstrating and saved a rare kind of stickleback minnow, but I was never going to come out, and I'd never talk again because people were like, you know, dishonest. And then you didn't take the gold." He smiled and sighed. "I had to, like, speak, man, and tell you how I felt."

Dunc stared. "Is your last name Davis?"

Milt nodded. "Cool—you know it."

"This wilderness area is named for you, to honor you."

"Oh, wow, groovy!"

"So now it's all over, and you can come out and be with the world again."

Milt shook his head. "Oh, no, man—I'd like, miss the tournament."

The boys looked at each other, then at Milt. "What tournament?"

"Every summer there's a checkers tournament. I don't want to miss it."

Amos coughed and looked at Dunc. "Milt, you're alone here."

Milt nodded.

"And you have this tournament yourself? You just play against yourself?"

Another nod. "Oh, man, like, last year it was really close. I almost won."

Slowly Amos set the bar of gold, which he'd been holding all this time, gently on the ground. He stood. "Well, Milt, we'd like to stay, but our parents and everybody will be looking for us and worrying."

Dunc nodded. "We really have to be going."

Milt moved, or seemed to move, and was standing between them and the water. Liquid movement. "Are you sure?"

They nodded.

"Well, if you, like, really *have* to go—take the boat and the bar of gold. A rafting group went through this morning. I saw them when I went back to check for any gear you might have lost. Maybe you can catch them."

He turned and dragged the rubber boat and the paddles to the water. "Over on the right, if you scrunch the boat a bit, it will slide under the rock and out into the river." He picked up the bar of gold and handed it to Amos.

"Are you sure of this?" Dunc asked.

"Yes," Amos said. "He is. Aren't you, Milt?"

Milt nodded. "It's the best checkers I've ever had—except for the tournament, of course."

"Of course." Amos took the bar and held it close to his chest.

"The gold is the least I can do."

"Of course."

"And the raft," Milt added. "You take the raft and paddles—you won them anyway, fair and square. If you stay with the river, you'll be out of the wilderness in three days, maybe less. I'll throw in some Spam and hash browns and a pan, too, and you can make it all, like, a picnic."

Dunc nodded to Amos. "All right, then—just this once."

Milt helped them load gear and punch the three-man raft down beneath the lip of rock leading to the outside. The boys held their breath and ducked under and came up next to the boat, and as Milt had said, they were in the river.

More important, the boat was in the edge of the current, and the swirling water caught it and started to tear it away. Amos threw the bar of gold into the boat, and the boys clawed their way up and over the side, and the river grabbed the boat and they were gone.

They looked back just in time to see Milt smile and wave at them and yell: "Watch out for the—"

And they rounded a bend and heard no more.

Chapter · 12

"It's like something out of a Mark Twain book," Dunc said.

The boys were lying against the sides of the boat. It was midday and the sun was hot, and the river scooted peacefully along, pushing the boat over riffles and occasional small rapids.

"Floating down the river on a warm day, a bar of gold—it could be a dream," Dunc finished. If the truth were known, he was having trouble keeping his eyes open. The sun warmed the rubber of the raft and made it feel like a warm bed.

"No—it's not like a dream." Amos dozed on the other side of the raft, one hand on the bar of gold. "If this was a dream, I'd be slamming my head through a wall or getting ripped to pieces by phones with teeth."

"Trappers," Dunc said.

"What?"

"The gold—it was for trappers. That's been bugging me since I saw the date. Then I remembered—all this country was first explored by fur trappers. The buyers used to carry gold and silver up the rivers to buy furs from the trappers. They probably hid it in the cave, then drowned in the river or got lost in a storm or something. Trappers—that's who owned the gold."

"It's ours now—at least, this bar."

Dunc nodded. "There it is—our college education."

"Right." Amos snorted. "You know how many Twinkies this will buy? Or phones? I could have phones lined on every wall of the house, stuck to the ceilings. I could buy a cellular phone and take it with me."

"They'll make us save it for college," Dunc interrupted. "Our parents."

Amos sighed. "Yeah."

There was a moment of silence, which led to another moment, then a full minute, and then five minutes. The raft bobbed down the river, the sun warmed the boys until their eyes were closed, and the past three days caught up with the sun and the gentle rolling of the raft, and they were asleep.

Dunc heard it first—a kind of muted hissing roar that cut into his sleep.

His eyes opened.

He looked around the raft. Nothing was changed. It was later in the afternoon, but they were still bobbing along, the sun beating down on them.

He closed his eyes and tried to get back to sleep.

A new sound cut in, and this time Amos opened his eyes as well as Dunc.

It was human voices.

The muted roar was a little louder now, and the current seemed to be traveling a bit faster, and mixed in were voices.

Yelling. They were yelling something.

Dunc raised his head to look at the shore. Amos sat up. There, not thirty yards away, stood Melissa Hansen.

"Melissa?" he said, and ducked immediately because he thought he was dreaming. He was pretty sure that if he saw Melissa in a dream, something bad would happen to him. Except that he wasn't dreaming. "Look, Dunc, it's Melissa. It's the raft trip—we caught up with them. I forgot that she was going on that raft trip. Oh, man, look—she's *waving* at me."

Dunc frowned. The background noise was louder now and made it hard to hear. "They're yelling something—what are they saying?"

Melissa stood in front of the group, and all of them, eight or ten including the guide, were jumping up and down yelling something, pointing down the river.

"Maybe they want us to paddle in to shore and join them," Amos said, nodding. "Sure. Melissa knows it's me and wants us to join their group."

"No." Dunc's voice grew cold and flat. "They're trying to warn us. Grab a paddle. We've got to get to shore—I just figured out what they're yelling." Dunc snatched up a paddle and started paddling. "It's falls—they're warning us about a falls. That's the sound, that roar."

Amos knew then, knew Melissa would not be waving, knew that even though it wasn't a dream, something bad was going to happen to him.

Something very bad.

He picked up the second paddle and started pulling at the water, matching strokes with Dunc, who was by now frantic. But he knew. He knew they weren't going to make shore.

The roar was close to deafening now, and the raft seemed to be gripped by a huge, angry fist. It shot down the middle of the river, around a sharp bend, and headed for the edge of what appeared to be a water cliff.

"We're going over!" Dunc screamed.

Amos nodded. Of course. He had known it all along. He looked back, caught one glimpse of Melissa and the rest of the rafting trip waving and screaming, and turned to the front just in time to see the world, the entire world, seem to disappear in front of and below them.

Of course, he thought—*of course we're going over.* How could it be any other way?

The bottom dropped out. He saw Dunc grab a plastic handle on the side of the raft, and he had a fleeting instant to clutch at one next to his hand. He missed, tried to grab the bar of gold, and missed that as well. He came up with a can of Spam and looked down over the tipping raft, down and down into a yawning, boiling, seething caldron of water as he fell away from the raft and Dunc, fell down and down and away to plummet at terminal velocity head down, still holding the can of Spam, into a world of thundering madness.

Chapter · 13

The dream seemed real. Amos was upside down, right side up, dragged and pushed and pulled and ripped and flattened. Somebody had him, grabbed him, held him down, and Melissa was leaning over him, leaning over him and down to—what? To kiss him? No. Not even in a dream—and then he heard a phone ringing.

One ring. Dimly, almost not there, a faint ring. But it was enough. Everything in him tensed, and he went for it. Classic form, rolling and to his feet, one leg down, the other up . . .

"Amos!"

. . . second leg down. Still well before the second ring, feet starting to pump, one hand out to get the phone, but something, something holding him back . . .

"Amos—wake up!"

. . . something had him, pulling him back and down, some enemy—he fought . . .

"Amos—"

His eyes opened. He was jammed into the corner of a hospital room, a sheet from the bed wrapped around his shoulders and legs, his head down, one hand up trying to reach a phone on a small table by the door.

"Amos, wake up."

He looked back, upside down through his armpit, to see Dunc lying in a bed nearby.

The phone rang again, and Dunc jumped from his bed. He answered it, then shook his head. "You've got the wrong room." He hung up and knelt next to Amos and helped him to his feet.

"Dunc?" Amos shook his head. "Are we in a hospital?"

Dunc nodded. "Just for observation. Everything is all right. Or will be."

"But what about the river, the falls, Milt—all that?"

"Good, you remember, then—I was worried.

You took a crack on your head under water, and I wasn't sure. The doctors said it would be fine, but you know me."

Amos closed his eyes and frowned, working at memory. "Gold—what happened to the gold bar?"

Dunc almost didn't have to answer. It was in his eyes. "You dropped it. Or missed it. When Melissa dragged you out of the water, you were holding a can of Spam."

"Melissa?" Amos stopped him. "She dragged me out?"

Dunc nodded. "Both of us. She climbed down next to the falls, and she was the first one to get to us. I was still conscious, but she had to work on you to bring you around."

"Work on me? How do you mean?"

"She did mouth-to-mouth on you."

"Melissa?"

Dunc nodded. "Of course, you didn't know it because you were unconscious from the head blow. They had a radio and called in a chopper —which wasn't very far away because they were still looking for us. They rushed us to the hospital—we were here within an hour."

"She kissed me?" Amos had stopped listening. "Melissa kissed me?"

"No. She gave you the breath of life. It's not the same. And you didn't know it. You didn't know anything until just now. The doctor said you have to keep a grip on the real world because of the blow on your head."

"Oh, man—I thought it was all a dream. Melissa kissed me, and I missed it!"

"You've got to control this, Amos—she doesn't even know your name. She just happened to rescue you. You've got to concentrate on real things, more positive things."

"Like losing the gold?" Amos asked.

"Well, no."

"Like crashing in a hang glider and getting kidnapped and covered with bat poop and nearly drowned and having you talk me out of playing checkers for more gold than there is in the whole world?"

"Well, not exactly." Dunc smiled. "I was thinking more of the two world records we set—no, three."

Amos was back on his bed, and he sat on the edge and looked at Dunc. "Longest flight for two boys our age."

Dunc nodded.

"What were the other two?"

"Highest flight for two boys, and . . ."

"And what?"

Dunc looked out the window, then back at Amos. "The only people ever to ride a rubber raft over Doom Falls."

"Doom Falls?"

"That's the name of the waterfall we went over. We're the only ones ever to go over Doom Falls and live."

Amos sighed and lay back on the bed. "She kissed me."

"Not really." Dunc shook his head. "Think of the records, Amos."

"Kissed me . . ."

"Amos."

"Melissa . . ."

"Amos."

Be sure to join Dunc and Amos in these other Culpepper Adventures:

The Case of the Dirty Bird

When Dunc Culpepper and his best friend, Amos Binder, first see the parrot in a pet store, they're not impressed—it's smelly, scruffy, and missing half its feathers. They're only slightly impressed when they learn that the parrot speaks four languages, has outlived ten of its owners, and is probably 150 years old. But when the bird starts mouthing off about buried treasure, Dunc and Amos get pretty excited —let the amateur sleuthing begin!

Dunc's Doll

Dunc and his accident-prone friend Amos are up to their old sleuthing habits once again. This time they're after a band of doll thieves! When a doll that once belonged to Charles Dickens's daughter is stolen from an exhibition at the local mall, the two boys put on their detective gear and do some serious snooping. Will a vicious watchdog keep them from retrieving the valuable missing doll?

Culpepper's Cannon

Dunc and Amos are researching the Civil War cannon that stands in the town square when they find a note inside telling them about a time portal. Entering it through the dressing room of La Petite, a women's clothing store, the boys find themselves in downtown Chatham on March 8, 1862—the day before the historic clash between the *Monitor* and the *Merrimac*. But the Confederate soldiers they meet mistake them for Yankee spies. Will they make it back to the future in one piece?

Dunc Gets Tweaked

Best friends Dunc and Amos meet up with Amos's cousin, Lash, when they enter the radical world of skateboard competition. When somebody "cops"—steals—Lash's prototype skateboard, the boys are determined to get it back. After all, Lash is about to shoot for a totally rad world's record! Along the way they learn a major lesson: *never* kiss a monkey!

Dunc's Halloween

Dunc and his best friend, Amos, are planning the best route to get the most candy on Halloween. But their plans change when Amos is slightly bitten by a werewolf. He begins scratching himself and chasing UPS trucks: he's become a werepuppy!

Dunc and the Flaming Ghost

Dunc's not afraid of ghosts, although Amos is sure that the old Rambridge house is haunted by the ghost of Blackbeard the Pirate. Then the best friends meet Eddie, a meek man who claims to be impersonating Blackbeard's ghost in order to live in the house in peace. But if that's true, why are flames shooting from his mouth?